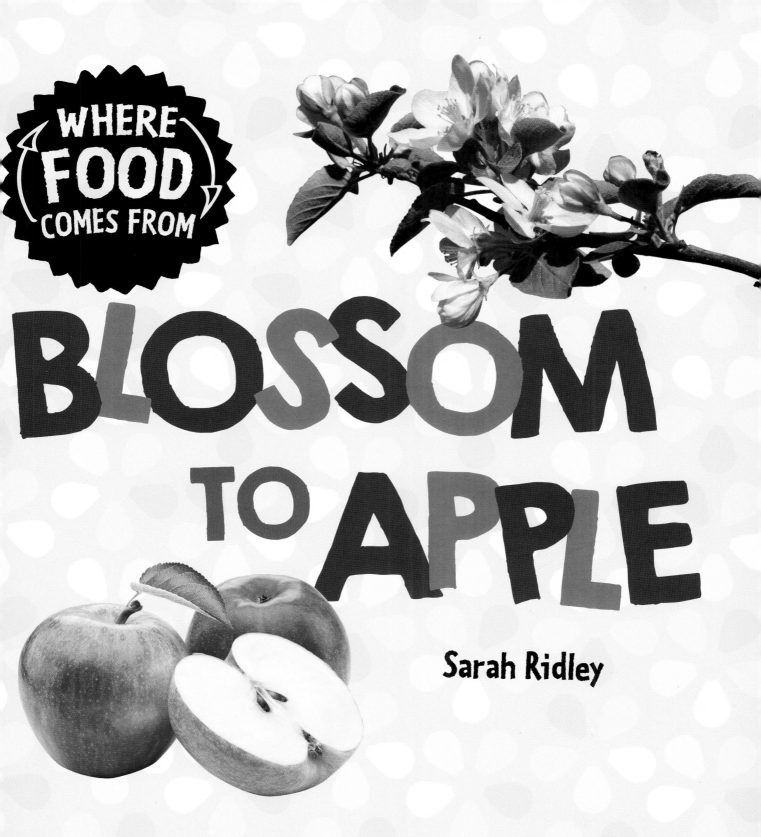

WHERE FOOD COMES FROM

BLOSSOM
TO APPLE

Sarah Ridley

CRABTREE
PUBLISHING COMPANY
WWW.CRABTREEBOOKS.COM

Published in Canada
Crabtree Publishing
616 Welland Avenue
St. Catharines, ON
L2M 5V6

Published in the United States
Crabtree Publishing
PMB 59051
350 Fifth Ave, 59th Floor
New York, NY 10118

Published in 2019 by Crabtree Publishing Company

First Published in Great Britain in 2018 by Wayland
Copyright © Hodder and Stoughton, 2018

Author: Sarah Ridley

Editors: Sarah Peutrill, Petrice Custance

Design: Matt Lilly

Proofreader: Ellen Rodger

Prepress technician: Margaret Amy Salter

Print coordinator: Katharine Berti

Every attempt has been made to clear copyright. Should there be any
inadvertent omission please apply to the publisher for rectification.

Printed in the U.S.A./082018/CG20180601

Photographs

Adisa/Shutterstock: 22. AGF photo/Superstock: 20. Viktoriia Chursina/
Shutterstock:5. Darkscott/Istockphoto: 3cr. Granville Davies/LOOP/Alamy:
18, 19t. Jacques Durocher/Shutterstock: 17, 24tr. Jens Gade/Istockphoto:
2, 14. Evgeny Karandaev/Shutterstock: 3cl. K Kulikov/Shutterstock: 15. V
J Matthew/Shutterstock: front cover t, 1t, 4, 24l. Mobi68/Dreamstime:
12. Christian Muelle/Shutterstock: 16. Pixelnest/Shutterstock: 13. Pulsar
Imagens/Alamy: 21. Red Helga/Istockphoto: 23. Red Stallion/Istockphoto: 7.
Edwin Remsberg/Alamy: 19b. Valentin Russanov/Istockphoto: 9. SOMMA/
Shutterstock: 3tl. Vasilyev/Shutterstock: 24bl. Katsiuba Volha/Shutterstock:
10. Valentyn Volkov/Shutterstock: front cover b, 1b. Lorraine Yates/Alamy: 8.
bligehan ylimaz/Istockphoto: 6.

Library and Archives Canada Cataloguing in Publication

Ridley, Sarah, 1963-, author
        Blossom to apple / Sarah Ridley.

(Where food comes from)
Includes index.
Issued in print and electronic formats.
ISBN 978-0-7787-5120-5 (hardcover).--
ISBN 978-0-7787-5131-1 (softcover).--
ISBN 978-1-4271-2168-4 (HTML)

    1. Apples--Development--Juvenile literature. 2. Apples--Juvenile
literature. I. Title.

SB363.R53 2018   j634'.11   C2018-902473-9
                                            C2018-902474-7

Library of Congress Cataloging-in-Publication Data
CIP available at the Library of Congress

CONTENTS

Apples are a tasty fruit. We eat them raw, cook them, and squash them to make juice.

But where do apples come from?

WHAT ARE APPLES?

Apples are the fruit of apple trees. They grow in gardens or **orchards**. Most big orchards belong to fruit farmers.

There are thousands of different varieties of apple tree. Their apples look and taste different.

APPLE FACT

Apple varieties have names. Here are a few: McIntosh, Red Delicious, Golden Delicious, Granny Smith, and Gala.

APPLE TREES

In winter, apple trees stand bare in the orchard or backyard.

APPLE FACT

Apple trees are **deciduous**, which means they drop their leaves in autumn. Evergreen trees keep their leaves over the winter.

This fruit farmer is **pruning** his apple trees.
He cuts off dead branches as well as branches
that are growing too close to each other.

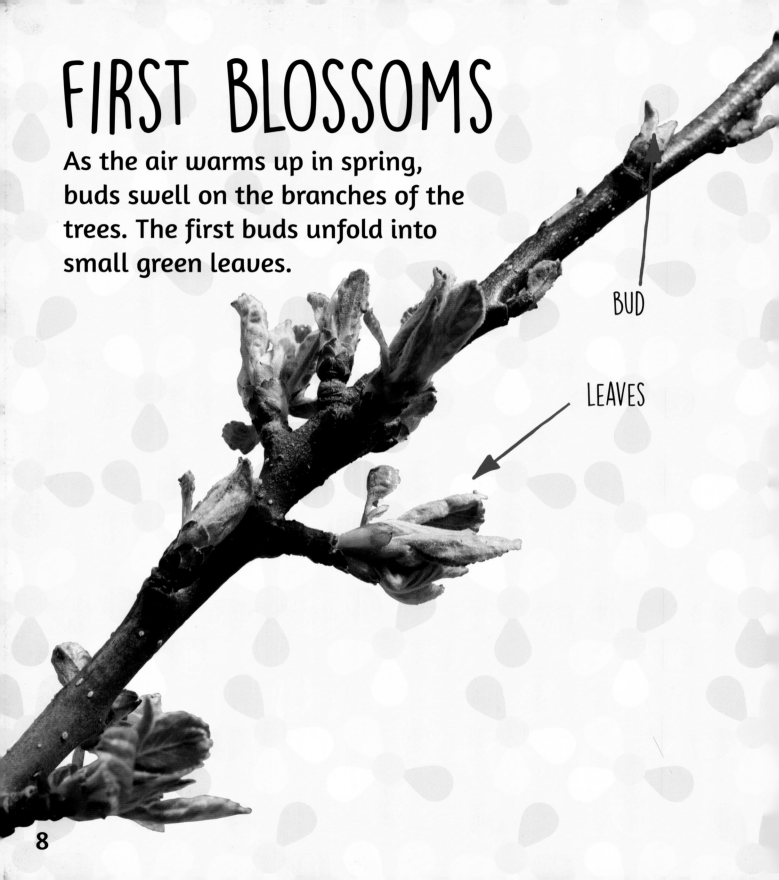

FIRST BLOSSOMS

As the air warms up in spring, buds swell on the branches of the trees. The first buds unfold into small green leaves.

BUD

LEAVES

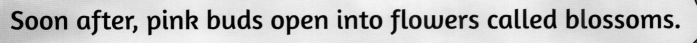

Soon after, pink buds open into flowers called blossoms.

WONDER WORD:
BLOSSOM

Blossom is another word
for the flowers of trees
or bushes, especially
fruit trees.

For a few weeks, apple trees are covered in blossoms. The blossoms contain a sugary food called nectar.

WONDER WORD:
NECTAR

Nectar is a sweet liquid made by plants to attract insects to their flowers.

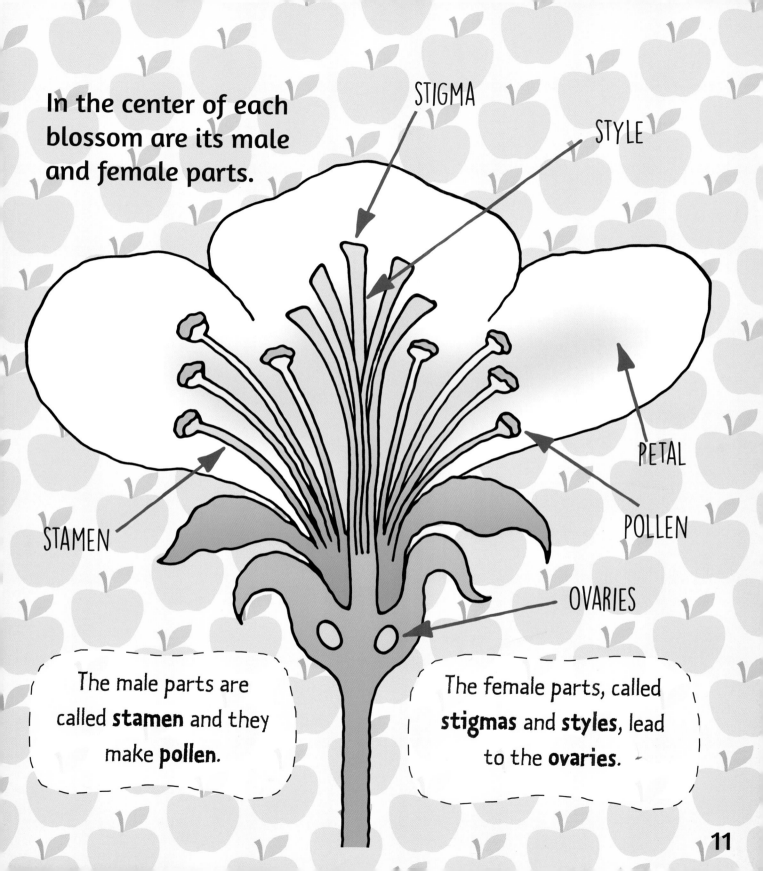

In the center of each blossom are its male and female parts.

STIGMA

STYLE

PETAL

POLLEN

STAMEN

OVARIES

The male parts are called **stamen** and they make **pollen**.

The female parts, called **stigmas** and **styles**, lead to the **ovaries**.

11

MAKING APPLES

On warm, dry days, apple trees buzz with the sound of bees. The bees fly from tree to tree, collecting nectar. Other insects collect the nectar, too.

As a bee sucks up nectar, pollen sticks to its hairy body. Some of the pollen brushes off onto the next blossom the bee visits, allowing pollination to happen.

WONDER WORD:
POLLINATION

Pollination takes place when the male part (pollen) of one flower reaches the female part of another, allowing it to make fruit and seeds.

13

Soon, the blossom petals fall to the ground. Where the blossom once was, tiny apples start to grow and swell.

APPLE FACT

In early summer, apple trees lose some of their smallest apples to allow the rest to grow well.

14

During the summer, the trees are covered in green leaves. The leaves make food for the trees using water, air, and sunlight. Water is soaked up under the ground by the trees' roots.

HARVESTING APPLES

The food that reaches the apples makes them grow bigger and bigger. Warmth from the Sun helps apples to become **ripe** in late summer and autumn.

Ripe apples will drop to the ground if farmers don't **harvest** them. An apple is ripe and ready for harvesting if it comes off the tree with a gentle twist.

Fruit farmers pay pickers
to harvest the apples.
It is a busy time.

APPLE FACT

Apple trees take four to
five years to produce their
first fruit.

Sometimes pickers need to use a ladder to reach the apples at the top of tall trees.

The pickers carefully place the apples in big crates or boxes.

Many fruit farmers send their apples to packing houses. There, apples are washed, sorted, and packed.

The apples are put into bags, boxes, or trays.

Farmers sell their apples to grocery stores or to factories where the apples are made into juice, pies, and other products.

HEALTHY APPLES

We buy apples and bring them home to eat. Apples help us stay healthy because they give us **nutrients**.

If you cut an apple in half you will see its seeds. You can grow an apple tree from a seed but most people plant small trees. Before long, the young apple tree will blossom and grow apples.

APPLE FACT

"An apple a day keeps the doctor away." Experts agree with this well-known phrase. They say that eating apples every day helps prevent illness while also helping people to **digest** food better.

23

GLOSSARY

deciduous Trees that lose their leaves at the end of their growing period

digest To break down food in the body

harvest To gather a crop

nutrients Natural substances found in foods that the body needs to function and stay healthy

orchard An area of land where fruit trees grow

ovaries The female part of a plant from which new plants grow

pollen The fine powder that is produced by the male part of a flower

prune To trim away dead or overgrown branches

ripe Ready to eat

stamen The part of a plant that produces pollen

stigma The part of a flower that receives pollen

style The part of a plant that connects the stigma to the ovaries

INDEX